SOLDATI DE SANGUE

SORROW'S QUEEN

ASHLEIGH GIANNOCCARO
MURPHY WALLACE

THE SOLDIERS OF BLOOD

Interconnected standalones that will push your limits, test your one-handed reading technique, and take you into a suspenseful world where men are domineering and dangerous, and their female counterparts are feisty and strong.

Are you ready to take the ride with us?

CHAPTER 1

Sorrow

I hate New York, every part of it. The entire state can fuck right off the damn map. I cannot believe the little bitch has been hiding in Queens. If her parents thought they'd be able to hide her forever, they're fools. I'm like a bloodhound when it comes to sniffing out the fox I'm hunting. She's running about town like there's no one nipping at her heels, going to school and having her nails done.

Naïve.

She's being hunted, and I am sick of the chase. I hate being here, the minute I have her we are leaving this hell-hole and, if I have my way, I'll never be back.

For the life of me, I can't wrap my head around this job. What about this girl is it that Marcus King could possibly want? Other than probably her baby teeth and virginity, I just don't get it. He's in his fifties, she turns eighteen in six weeks. There are other, much easier ways of catching a young wife—it's not like he doesn't have women throwing themselves at his feet already.

Why make me chase the one that wants nothing to do with him, halfway across the country? Ever heard of mail-order brides? You can get a real hottie from Russia that can't talk back because she doesn't know English. That would be easier than this.

My burner phone buzzes in the center console of the car. It can only be Arthur or one of my brothers. I pick it up and click on the message icon.

Check on Gareth. It's Arthur.

I'm in Queens trying to catch King's future wife. Ask Lance to stop by. I type a quick reply.

It crushes me that I can't be there for my brother right now; at such a fragile time in his life. That's another strike against Queen bitch and just one more reason to hate her. These next few days can't go by quick enough. I have half a mind to tie her up, gag her, and throw her in my trunk for the journey back to

Arthur's house.

The bell rings, signaling the end of the school day. I keep an eye out for her. I am not missing my chance to grab the little Queenie from Queens and get the fuck out of town.

The phone vibrates in my hand before I can put it down.

There's a wedding in six weeks — she better be there. Do not let me down, Tristan.

There it is, the unspoken truth. Arthur is just waiting for me to fail him. One mistake and you're on his list, his eyes on your every move. No room to mess up. I won't do it again. Letting him down isn't an option, I am going to prove myself to him.

I still beat myself up over what happened a few years ago. I was new to the Soldati di Sangue, and I had one job; to be the lookout during the takedown of Marcus King's greatest enemy. I was pissed off and wanted to prove myself, so I left my post to assist with the hunt. Because of that, Kay ended up with two gunshot wounds and a knife in the leg. He almost died. The only reason that Arthur didn't kill me is that Kay convinced him not to. I still don't know exactly why he did it, but ever since then I've been busting my ass to make it up to him; to all of them.

I watch Queen Sophie as she exits the school gates. She turns left and heads right toward where I am parked, just far enough away that no one will notice me. I have been watching her for two weeks; I know she will walk alone, reading a book. She has no friends here—she's not like these kids. I may not like her, but that doesn't mean she doesn't affect me. Her plaid skirt is two inches too short, and the matching headband that keeps her raven locks off her pretty face makes her look like jailbait.

Fuck. She is *jail bait.*

My cock gets hard and I shift a little to adjust myself.

That Catholic school girl look might be what Marcus is after—bet your life if she wasn't a kid, or my mark, I'd push her up against the wall and have my way with her. Standing against my car now, the afternoon sun broiling me, I wait until she is two steps away, then I open the back door of my rented BMW. I made sure the child lock is on, so once she's in she can't get out again.

"Hello, Queen," I say, stepping right in front of her.

She crashes into me, and I grab her wrist. Before she can scream or kick up a fuss, she's in the car, and

I'm slamming the door closed. People are so slow to realize when they're in danger—when the predator is right beside them and, still, they can't smell it.

Her book falls into the dirty gutter water running beside my car, and I don't bother trying to save it. I need to move quickly before anyone sees us or hears her. I get into the driver's side of the car and start it, quickly merging into the after-school traffic.

Sophie is screaming and banging on the glass partition between us. I chose a chauffeur car for this exact reason. I don't want to get all scratched up. Those talons on her fingers would do some serious damage. She's kicking the glass like a maniac now.

It's a long drive all the way across the country. We don't fly with people we've kidnapped—it's risky. We're in for a twenty-one-hour drive without stopping, so the next two days will give her enough time to cool off, or pass out. I turn up the music to drown out her wailing and get on the freeway.

As soon as I know we're not being followed, I pick up the burner phone and call Arthur.

"Tristan."

He greets me in his usual flat tone. Not a hint of emotion in his voice. There's no way to tell if he's murderous or happy.

"I have the girl. She's a bit feral, but it's a long drive. She'll have time to calm down." I look in the mirror at her. "Should I expect trouble from the cops?"

"No, her family won't report her missing. You should have clean sailing all the way here."

"See you in two or three days."

"I'll be waiting," he answers before cutting the call.

She is no longer screaming like a banshee. Instead, she is trying to murder me with her eyes. Her death glare is so cute it's almost funny. I laugh at her in the mirror. The penny has obviously dropped, I watch her digging in her backpack for her phone. She can call anyone she wants; no one is coming to save her. This arrangement was made between her father and Marcus. She doesn't get a choice; her parents will not step in and stop it.

That would be suicide.

"Daddy," I hear her cry into the phone.

I turn the music down, listening to her side of the exchange.

"What's going on? You told me that you'd fix this," she sobs.

"He's a sick old pervert!" Her voice rises an octave.

"I'll kill myself. I'm telling you now. I will slit my

wrists before I marry that wrinkly old bastard."

She listens for a few moments, her breaths heavy and ragged.

"I hate you! I fucking hate you!" she screams before hurling her phone against the glass that separates us.

She cries now, the tantrum replaced with emotional sobs. They get under my thick skin as I listen to her breaking. The problem with being born into the underworld is you have no choice, your family is a part of this. Her birthright was always to be promised to a powerful man to strengthen family ties. Her father just picked a really shitty one for her. The way her eyes beg me to save her plays into the small soft part of me that isn't completely lost to what I do for a living. For a second I consider letting her get away, but that would be like signing my own death certificate.

Not delivering isn't an option.

Eventually, she lies down on the backseat, I can still hear her sniffling, but I can't see her face. Taking the chance, I turn the radio up again and work on creating strong barriers around my emotions. There's no room for feelings in this job, because if you have empathy for one person, how can you turn around and kill the next one? The afternoon turns into the haziness of dusk and soon the sun is gone completely. The streetlights and black sky are calling me home. Downing two energy drinks and shifting around in my seat, I settle myself for the long drive to the designated motel where we will rest for the night.

My eyelids have been heavy for the last hundred miles, and the shitty pink motel sign is the most welcome sight in the early hours of the morning. We'll stop here for a few hours of sleep and grab a shower and a hot breakfast. I park the car and flash my lights three times. After a few minutes, the desk clerk, Larry, comes out and hands me the key to room nine through the window.

"Sorrow. Haven't seen you in these parts for years. I was surprised when they said it was you coming." he says, smiling at me with his missing front tooth and saggy eyelids.

"Good to see you, Larry," I say, taking the key. "You busy tonight? This one might make noise."

"Only one room full and it's upstairs at the other end of the corridor. You should be good. If anyone complains, I'll deal with it."

"Thanks, man," I say.

"See you for breakfast then?" he asks me, shoving his hands in the pockets of his grubby jeans.

"Sure thing."

He nods and disappears back into his office. I move the car so it's parked right in front of room nine, out of sight of the road and passers-by. I know she's awake, but she's still laying down. I open the glass that separates us, just enough that I can talk to her.

"We're stopping for the night. I'd really like if this wasn't a fucking ordeal, so let's go inside like civilized adults, please. No one will hear you scream, and if you run, I will shoot you. The caretaker is paid very well to turn a blind eye, so you're not getting saved here. Think you can be a big girl and walk the three feet to the door?"

She's sitting up now, looking at me with tired, swollen eyes.

"If I say no?"

"Then I grab you, put you over my shoulder and drag you inside, anyway."

She swallows, then licks her dry lips.

"There's no option where you win, there's just an

easy way and a hard way to do what I want."

"I'm not going to do anything you want, so I guess there'll be a lot of hard-way going on." The death stare is back.

Jesus, really?

I would rather be doing anything than this job, I swear.

"Fine," I sigh.

CHAPTER 2

Queen

He opens the car door and before I can lunge at him, he grabs me by my hair and tugs so hard I feel the strands pulling out of my scalp. I start to kick, scratch, and scream, but he's bigger than me. He's also strong and as solid as a fucking brick wall. Nothing I do is going to move him.

He drags me out of the car by my hair and in one swift move he hoists me over his shoulder. My head hanging upside down right by his backside, he smells like the breeze of the Mediterranean and the leather of his jacket. He's awfully good looking for a kidnapper, I always thought stranger danger would be uglier.

He wasn't wrong—there's no escaping this. I have known since my fifteenth birthday that this day would come. But I refuse to go down without a fight. I may not get to decide what my future holds, but I sure as hell am not going to just give myself over to Marcus King willingly and with no fight. The door closes behind us, and he turns on a light, but still doesn't put me down.

"You can put me down," I say between gritted teeth.

I wiggle, trying to get free of the death grip he's got on me. With that, he just lets go, letting me slump down to the floor with no help or warning. He steps over me to put the small bag he's carrying on the floor. From my spot on the ground, I contemplate running, but when I look around the room carefully, I am willing to bet my life none of the other motel rooms look like this on the inside.

The door is steel reinforced; I know because my dad has the same one for his office. The windows are all shuttered from the inside and resemble a bank once the alarm has gone off. The smooth white floors look sterile and there is minimal furniture in the room. One bed, a single chair. A small table and a wardrobe. It's all very modern and clean, nothing like the dingy outside of the motel. This room isn't for guests.

I don't know who he is, but I'm sure he's one of them. The first time I met Marcus, he was with a man called Arthur, and some of his 'men'. That was the day my father traded me in a business deal. This guy wasn't there that day, but I'd bet money on it he works for them.

"What's your name?" I ask him, pulling myself up off the floor.

My body is stiff and achy from sleeping in the car. He doesn't answer me and his behavior, his disinterest in the fact that he's just ripped me away from everything I've ever known, pisses me off. Catching him off guard, I run to where he is standing, removing his shirt.

"What is your name!" I scream as I shove him.

Not that it did any bit of good though; he didn't even budge. I stand rooted to the spot, paralyzed by his fierce stare. As terrified as I am, I try my best not to let it show. After a moment, his face relaxes.

"You don't need to know my name," he answers, pulling off his dark jeans. "Go to bed. We're getting out of here as soon as the sun is up."

He climbs onto one side of the bed, rolls onto his side, and closes his eyes. I want to know his name. If he's going to ruin my life, I might as well know what to call him.

It's easier to catch flies with honey than vinegar.

I can hear my mother's voice in my head. Walking softly over to the side of the bed closest to me, I climb on and kneel next to him.

"I want to know your name. Please?" I ask, softly.

He sits up and glares at me.

"Well, I want to go to sleep," he barks out. "Apparently neither of us are going to get what we want."

What a dick. There goes the whole honey/vinegar theory.

"Where am I supposed to sleep?" I ask, I am *not* about to sleep in this bed with him.

"It's a big bed, Queen, you can have that whole side."

"I'm not getting into bed with a stranger who's name I don't know."

"Sorrow!" he shouts, but the anger leaves his face and his tone after a few seconds. "People call me Sorrow. Are you satisfied?"

"No, that's not an actual name."

"It is. Please, can we just get some sleep?"

"Why do people call you that?"

"Because I'm a sad motherfucker. Now, for the love of God, sleep." He rolls over again, huffing out a sigh.

I sit there, my aching body ready to sleep, but my mind is spinning with questions. Eventually, I get off the bed and go into the bathroom. After I pee and wash my face, I crawl onto the empty side of the bed and lie as still as I can.

"Do you know Marcus?" I ask him after I've been laying down for several minutes.

I'm testing whether he's asleep yet. I've been listening to his breathing, but I can't tell.

"Yes."

"Is he going to hurt me?"

"Probably." I open my mouth to talk, but he interrupts me. "I might hurt you first, however, if you don't shut the fuck up and go to sleep."

I stare at the ceiling until I hear soft snores coming from him. Moving carefully and quietly, I climb out of bed and crawl over to his bag. I don't know what I expect to find, but as I dig through his things, I'm disappointed at the fact that there isn't a weapon or anything else that would have helped me get away from him.

All that's in the damn bag is clean boxer shorts, a clean t-shirt, mouthwash and a book. Surprising for a paid assassin, but also not, I suppose. He wouldn't expect me to try to hurt him, I guess. Defeated, that's all I feel, slumped on the floor of this strange motel room.

"There's nothing in there to kill me with. Not even a plastic spoon, Queen," he says, not opening his eyes.

I don't like the way he calls me Queen; it makes my stomach flip and my skin tingle.

"And if you do manage to kill me, the wrath of eight angry murderers will rain down on you like a hurricane, so get in the bed and go the fuck to sleep—please."

Dragging myself off the floor, I climb on the bed, lie flat on my back and stare at the white ceiling.

"I wasn't going to try to kill you." I say a few minutes later, thinking he'd gone back to sleep.

"Really?" He says, the sarcasm dripping from his tongue.

"I wanted to kill myself. I don't want to marry Marcus, I'm afraid of him."

"You should be." He doesn't sugarcoat the reality I am about to be thrown into. "But, you should rather kill him, than yourself—suicide is stupid."

"I don't think it is."

"It is. Selfish and stupid."

"So are arranged marriages," I hiss, rolling over so I'm facing his back.

"We live in a selfish world, Queen." He really is a sad motherfucker. "Please go to sleep. I'm not your friend, I can't chat with you. You're my job."

"You have a shit job."

"I swear to God if you don't shut up, I will gag you."

"I just—" Before I can finish my thought, he's up out of bed. He unlocks the wardrobe with a code and returns with a roll of duct-tape. I move up on the bed, in a sad attempt to scramble away from him, but he straddles my body, pinning me down. Using his teeth, he tears off a strip of tape, then grabs my face, squashing my cheeks so I have fish-lips before smoothing the tape over my mouth. Sealing it shut, silencing me. Then he takes my wrists, which were pinned by his knees, and tapes them tightly together. Leaning forward, he whispers against my cheek.

"Go to sleep, please."

Before he gets up, puts the tape away and locks the wardrobe again. I wonder what else is in there?

CHAPTER 3

Sorrow

It's a very long drive from Queens back to Arthur's place—it's exponentially longer when doing it with a petulant teenage girl in the back seat. Thankfully, she finally fell back to sleep. She was up most of the night thinking. Her thoughts and worries were so loud they were keeping me awake. I think she was trying to tire me out so she could get away.

My phone starts buzzing from the center console, and I pick it up to see who it is.

Arthur.

What the fuck does he want now? I just gave him an update three hours ago, just before leaving the hotel.

"Yeah," I say, answering the phone.

"Something's come up. Sophie's parents just signed their death warrants, the dumb fucks."

Arthur goes on to explain that they never had any intention of giving her away to Marcus. Apparently, they were dumb enough to think that tricking him would actually work. They promised her to him and went on with their lives, acting as if they were actually going to follow through with it to keep Marcus off of their backs.

Then, the moment they found out that the time had come, they cried abduction and the authorities issued an Amber Alert to get her back.

"Make sure you stick to back roads and small towns. Marcus doesn't know yet. At least not to my knowledge; he hasn't come beating my door down anyhow. But Tristan, now more than ever you need to be smart. Stay alert. No distractions. If anything happens, I want you to find a place to lie low and contact me as soon as you can. Got it?"

"Got it. I'll get her there as promised."

"See you in a few days."

The line disconnects as Arthur hangs up the phone. What has already felt like an eternity will now take longer to get her delivered.

"Who was that?"

Jesus. She startled me. And that is something that never happens.

"Was it your friend? Was it Arthur?"

How the fuck does she know about Arthur? I keep my face neutral, but something tells me that she knows she got a reaction out of me. When I don't answer, she drops it.

We manage to make it out of the immediate area and drive for several hours before we find trouble. I noticed a line of cars backing up the road just before the exit to get onto the main highway. I manage to get us turned around and off in a new direction without causing alarm.

Unfortunately, Sophie is too smart for her own good.

"Why are you turning around?" she asks, knowing damn well why.

I don't answer her. I'm not a liar, so I just won't say anything.

"They're looking for me, aren't they? My parents? The police?"

She pulls herself upright and starts banging on the window and screaming at the top of her lungs, trying to get anyone to hear. I wait until we are out of view of any witnesses and slam on my breaks. She goes flying forward and slams into the divider between us with a scream.

"Ouch! What the hell?" She says as I turn around to face her.

"Listen to me! No one is going to find you. Do you understand that? Your idiot parents fucked up, and they're good as dead. So even if you do get *rescued* you won't have any parents to go home to, and you will end up with an even more pissed off Marcus in the end, anyway."

Before I even stop talking, the tears are pouring down her face and I'm chiding myself for being such a fucking bastard. I take a deep breath and put the car back into drive. We need to get out of here. There isn't anyone around that I can see, but I don't want to chance someone seeing us from inside of their house and reporting it.

It took me about forty-five minutes to figure out the best way to get us back on track. I stopped once along the way to hot-wire a new vehicle for us to get away in; a black Tahoe. The person who I'm taking it from should be grateful. I left the Beemer behind with the key in the ignition.

I had to stop at a service station to fill up and prayed like hell that Sophie wouldn't create a problem for me. I think I broke something in her back there. She hasn't made a peep since. I feel like a big piece of shit but, honestly, the quicker she comes to terms with her future the better; because it's not fucking changing.

I grabbed some snacks and supplies from the store. I'm sure she's hungry. When I get back into the truck, I turn to her again.

"I got us some food, if you're hungry?"

She doesn't look at me or respond in any way.

"Last chance, Queen. Otherwise, I'm going to eat every last bit of it. And I don't know when we'll be stopping next. Could be hundreds of miles until then."

Her shoulders dip in defeat as she raises her eyes to meet mine.

"If you can behave, I'll even let you sit up front with me; where the big kids get to sit."

That last comment earns me a death stare, and I know then that I didn't completely crush her spirit.

"Give me a few minutes to get us down the road before we do a Chinese fire drill; that way no one sees you."

We make it about a hundred miles down the road with minimal conversation. But her attitude changed slightly the further we drove. She thinks I am a fool. That I haven't noticed the way she's been looking at me. I can see those little cogs turning inside her head—she's trying to seduce me.

She obviously watches way too much drivel on TV to think that's how it actually works. She plays with the sleeve of her shirt and looks up at me from under those long dark lashes. I understand more and more now why she's the one Marcus chose. I'd have cradle snatched her too if I had his money and power. She's going to be the perfect little Queen for Mr. King.

Just as I'm about to call her out on it, my phone buzzes again. I look at the screen and I see a message from Lance.

Don't come. Not safe.

What happened? I text back to him.

Her parents must have given them Arthur's name. Guess they thought that was safer than giving them Marcus.

Well, they thought wrong.

Fuck. My phone buzzes again.

Arthur wants you to find a place to lie low until he can get you a free pass home.

Thanks. I respond.

I pull over on the side of the road and look up hotels in the area. We're in the middle of nowhere, so I am not expecting any results. We may have to continue driving and check again.

We luck out, if that's what you want to call it, when a small B&B pops up in the results. It's the *only* place that popped up and it's about 30 miles from here. The place doesn't have a website, email address or a cell phone number, just a good old landline.

Definitely a plus.

"Change of plan, Queen. We're going to be lying low a little longer than expected."

"Don't try anything cute," I growl at her as we take the steps up to the B&B.

It's in a small, nondescript town, way off the radar of the real world. I need a proper night's sleep. My head has been pounding for hours, and I'm hungry for something that isn't a service station snack. I'm sure we're safe to hide out here until some of the heat dies down. Arthur must have some sort of plan to deal with this, to get the media and police to shut it down.

"I mean it Queen, don't pull anything stupid. Just smile and let me deal with this. Or I swear the duct tape will come out again."

She gives me a half scowl as we wait for the door to open. An old man with greying hair and a walking stick opens up the door and greets us.

"You must be the lad who called about a room?" he says with a smile.

"Yes, we're a little later than expected, but we took the scenic route. Wanted to soak in the countryside as much as we could."

I nearly choke on the banal words as they come out of my mouth. It's nothing like the words that get thrown around between my brothers and me.

"No problem, come on in, I'd offer to carry your bags, but I'm eighty-seven so you can get them yourselves," he says and I can see the utter mortification on Queen's face.

She doesn't like roughing it, she's a spoiled little brat. The entrance is bright and clean, but definitely old. It smells like cinnamon and lavender, and I can already tell we will be safely hidden here for a short while.

"'This is your room," he opens the door at the far

end of the hall, then hands me the key. "My wife serves breakfast at eight, and there's lunch on the back porch at one if you don't mind eating with us old farts. Dinner is in the dining room around seven each evening. If you need anything, holler—loud because we're both a little deaf."

I plaster on the best smile that I can and usher Sophie into the room.

"That's perfect, thank you. We will see you for dinner this evening. I think we're going to take a siesta, we're both tired after the long drive."

He winks at me with a knowing smile; he thinks I'm trying to get lucky with my girl.

She's not my girl, and getting lucky isn't an option on this job.

I roll my eyes and lock the door, pocketing the key and turning around to see Sophie looking out the window that faces the most immaculate back garden. The rows and rows of rose bushes, and the bubbling fountain enchant her.

Roses have thorns, and water can drown you.

I am less enchanted, but still appreciate beauty when I see it. I put down the small bag that contains the supplies I bought us both for traveling and survey my surroundings. It's more exposed than I'd like with the enormous windows and French doors that open up to the outside. Keeping her under control here is going to be hard. I might have to play along with her silly games to keep her distracted. I can't have her running off into the wilderness.

I really don't have time to catch her again.

"I am going to have a shower, don't do anything stupid Queen," I say, locking the French doors and removing the key.

She shouldn't be able to escape, the windows only open really high up, I'd hear her before she made it out that way.

"You mean like try to escape, or tell the deaf old man that you kidnapped me so that I can be sold as a child bride?" she says with sass and a devilish glint in her eyes. "I wouldn't dare."

She shakes her head and sighs, collapsing into a wing-back chair by the window.

"I am not a fool, Sorrow. I would rather not die, or have the shit beat out of me before my wedding. If I'm going to die, I want the satisfaction of deciding when and how."

"You're not going to kill yourself. Don't act like a child."

"You never know what I might do."

God, she's infuriating.

"In that case, come here." I grab her arm and drag her into the big en suite bathroom behind me.

"Sit." I growl, pushing her down onto the closed toilet. "You want to act like a child, I'll sit you in time out like a fucking child."

She doesn't answer me, her eyes tell me everything her perfect pink lips won't. I strip out of my clothes while the water warms up, relieved to remove the sweat and dirt of the day, and let my clothing fall into a pile on the floor.

I can see her reflection in the glass of the shower, she's staring at me. Not directly, no she's trying not to look, but she likes what she sees enough that she can't not. Her cheeks are flushed red, and she's trying hard not to move.

"Stop staring Queen, I know what you're thinking."

Her face glows beet red. I caught her ogling me and she's embarrassed.

"You have no idea what I'm thinking."

She tries to be sassy, but her voice waivers and she swallows the last words. Turning to face her, naked and exposed, I know I am intimidating her—but I am also breaking all sorts of rules.

She won't make eye contact with me; she won't look at me. Turning her head so that she's looking at the wall beside her, she avoids me.

"What's the matter Queen, have you never seen a penis before?" I don't know why I am pushing this, or why the fact that she's uncomfortable makes me so hard. "You can look, I am not ashamed of what God gave me."

She looks up at me now, her eyes locked on mine. When I see the tear falling down her cheek, I realize how close to the truth I am. Her bottom lip quivers and she closes her eyes.

"You've never seen a man naked, have you?"

She shakes her head and clasps her hands together. I'm angry in that moment, at her for the teasing comments and touches, the sassy, flirty talk—and I am angrier at myself for what I have done.

"Well, keep your eyes closed then, because you're not leaving this bathroom until we've both showered. I can't trust you to be alone."

My words sound harsher than I want as I walk away from her and into the steaming hot shower.

Fuck it, this girl is going to make me lose my damned mind before I get rid of her.

Chapter 4

Queen

If I can get him to like me, then maybe he won't give me to Marcus—this was my hare-brained plan. I cooked it up somewhere between nothing and nowhere as we drove, dodging roadblocks and search parties looking for me. Sorrow is clever, he's not going to get caught, no one will ever find me unless he wants me to be found.

He's naked and standing right there in front of me, not even trying to hide himself. I want to look, but I also don't. I shouldn't have teased; he can see straight through me. I've never even seen a boy my own age naked, let alone a large man who looks like he was chiseled from stone by God himself.

My father kept me in a gilded cage. I attend an all-girl's school. No parties, no boys, no friends. My internet and social media are monitored all the time, even if I was curious there's no way I could satisfy that curiosity without being caught—and punished.

I was to remain *pure* for my husband. Now, I'm sitting here on the toilet like a fool, faced with his penis standing up like a soldier at attention. There's a metal ring through the tip, and I wince just imagining how painful that must have been to get.

I know the biology of sex, because they taught us in school with some very basic drawings, but here, faced with that thing, I am questioning the mechanics of it. I'm not sure how it would fit where it's supposed to go.

My skin is clammy from the steam, and the blush I can't seem to get a control on. Averting my eyes as it gets harder and harder, and when he catches me looking at him under the steam of hot water, he gets this sick smile on his face.

It terrifies me.

Sorrow's eyes change, and my knees tremble where I'm resting my elbows on them. It's like he sees my fears and wants to make me face them. He's frightening and comforting in a single glance.

Deep in those menacing eyes, I can see the sadness he wears, like a badge of honor. I see it, because I feel it in myself. The agony in me recognizes the agony in him.

In this moment, staring at him, while he fists his cock—tugging and pulling it—his veins protrude from underneath his skin, drawing a roadmap down his arm. I almost don't see what he's doing. But I do see him. I look inside him and understand what he's doing. Sorrow is trying to hurt me, because he's hurting.

I've heard people talk about guys doing this. I've never imagined it to be quite like what is happening in front of me. He's not my captor, my kidnapper, or my enemy. No, he's just like me. Right now, he's being a massive jerk, playing with my innocence, using it against me. His already enormous dick is engorged. When I look down at it, I can see the dark red tip, bulging, heavy with whatever it is that makes a penis hard.

I shouldn't be looking at this, I shouldn't be watching him—I certainly should not like what I'm seeing. Biting my lip, I try to hide my fascination. He sees it; he knows that he's showing me something I have no business seeing. I find my voice, and my ability to think.

"Please stop."

"No one is making you watch, Queen," he says, and that devil smile grows wider. "You can look away anytime. But I think you like what you see."

He's rendered me speechless again, and I close my eyes.

"Queen, my hand feels so good, but I bet it would feel even better with your lips wrapped around me."

My what? Oh, God, that's disgusting.

"I'd be gentle, let you set the pace before I fucked your throat raw." My face burns with embarrassment just imagining the things he's saying. "You know, Marcus will expect you to suck his dick, he's going to use every part of your innocent little body to pleasure himself."

I gag thinking about Marcus King's penis. I wonder if it's impressive like Sorrow's or if it's old and disgusting like the rest of him.

"I could teach you how to make your husband happy."

"I'd rather you teach me how to kill him and get away with it." I say, trying desperately to diffuse some tension that fills the small room.

Sorrow chuckles at my response.

"I'll teach you anything you want to learn if you climb in here and suck my dick right now."

I can't do this; I can't be in here with him like that.

He's making my body react in strange ways I can't control. His nakedness has rendered my usually sharp mind useless, there's a fog of desire and disgust that won't lift. It's thick, like the steam in the bathroom.

"Come on, you know you want to. Besides, you need a shower too. Are you scared, little Queen?" He keeps going, as I stare at him. "The big bad cock has you afraid? Where's all that fight you had when I took you?"

I can't think of a single thing to say to him, because some small corner of my non-functioning brain is entertaining his stupidity. I look at the floor, desperate to escape that intense look in his eyes.

"Ahh," he moans loudly, making me look up at him.

Just in time to see him pulling hard on his cock, forcing ribbons of white liquid to spurt from it, landing all over the shower glass. I die a little inside and stand up, turn around and face the wall while I try to catch my breath.

"Too late, I wasted it all now. Don't worry. You can taste it next time."

I hear the shower door swing open and I hold my breath. Sorrow fills the room like the steam, sucking away the air and making it hard to breathe. He's an imposing presence, and I'm both drawn to and terrified of him.

Make him like you, Sophie. If he likes you, he might save you.

I keep telling myself the same thing—I need to win over the monster, so that I don't have to face an even worst one. Turning around slowly, he's now standing there with a fluffy white towel wrapped around his waist.

"Your turn, Queen. I'd get in before all the hot water is finished," he says with a smirk.

Swallowing the lump in my throat, I just stand there with my arms crossed over my fully clothed chest as he takes a seat on the toilet where I was sitting a few moments ago.

"Off you go. We both know you can't be trusted; I have to watch you." The way he says it, the words laced with threats, makes me feel warm inside. "I promise I've seen everything you're hiding before."

He mocks my childish innocence and I wish I had been more rebellious, that I'd at least had a boyfriend. Kissed a boy—anything—that could help me right now. But I am so far out of my depth that I am going to drown in spectacular fashion.

"Stop acting like a child. Do not make me pull those clothes off and shove you in the shower." He growls at me, baring his teeth like a rabid animal. "I'm tired and hungry. My fuse is short, little Queen."

Frozen with fear, I stand there with my lip trembling and tears stinging the corners of my eyes. I have never been naked in front of anyone, besides my mother and my nanny as a child. I don't look like the bikini girls in magazines; I don't like what I see when I'm naked—why would he? I stare at him, challenging his inner beast to carry out his threats, because I can't do what he's asking.

"It's like that, is it?" I gasp when he stands up quickly, stepping right in front of me. So close I can see the water droplets rolling down the tight skin that wraps the muscles of his chest.

"You can't make me." I find my voice beneath the fear.

"Oh, little Queen. I can, and I will." He walks around me like a hyena circling its prey, laughing and throwing his head back. "You see, until I hand you over to Marcus, you are mine to do with as I please. And I'm getting tired of being nice and getting nothing but sass in return. My patience is wearing very thin with you."

I glance to the locked door, and then to the small window.

"I'll make sure you can never get away from me. This is my job, Queen. I take things, things that don't belong to me. I kill people that get in my way, and when I am angry, I blow shit up. You don't want me to get angry. I suggest you take off your clothes before I do. Because if I'm the one who has to do it, you won't get them back until we leave this place—and dinner could be awkward without them."

"Why? Why are you doing this?"

"Because I enjoy it," he says, coming right up into my face now. "One last chance."

I can't do it. Even if I wanted to listen to him, my body won't cooperate with my head.

"My way it is then."

I squeeze my eyes closed, forcing my unshed tears to roll down my cheeks as I heave short, heavy breaths of air into my lungs.

"Arms up."

He barks the command my childhood nanny would say when I stood next to the bathtub, right before she would yank my dress up over my head. Just like Sorrow does now.

I can't open my eyes; I'm afraid of what I'll see in his. I try to cover myself, folding my arms over my too-big-for-my-frame breasts. I'm hyperventilating, I can feel the blood draining from my head as a finger traces a line down my spine.

He stops, hooking it into the strap of my bra, and somehow with just a single movement the clasp snaps open. He's closer to me now, standing over me, even with my eyes closed I can feel him looking at me.

"Drop it," he whispers, and I feel his breath tickle the skin on my neck, goosebumps tingle across my body as I let my arms fall to my sides.

The satin and lace bra falling to the floor without a sound.

"Good, Queen."

His voice whistles along my naked skin again as my knees shake, as his hands skim slowly down my sides, barely touching me. It's the same as when you put your hand over a candle and get licked by the flame.

Delightfully painful.

Biting the inside of my cheek, it's getting harder to keep my eyes closed. I almost—almost want to see the look on his face, but I don't. As he curls his cold fingers into the band of my underwear, I hold my breath, tense every part of my body, and wait for him to strip away the last shred of innocence and dignity I have.

I whisper a silent prayer in my mind—because I know that I will not escape this man with one part of my soul or body intact.

"Get in the shower, Queen, don't make me hurt you. This body is too perfect to be marked with my anger."

CHAPTER 5

Sorrow

God, she's magnificent, unspoiled perfection. Pure innocence.

We have been stuck in this B&B for two weeks now. Arthur says moving her isn't safe. Her future husband has too many enemies, and the national news made sure that every one of them knew his beloved was missing.

Now there is a huge reward being offered throughout the crime community for her safe return. Her parents are fools—soon to be dead fools. Her father is a stupid, white-collar criminal. He has never felt the stickiness of blood between his fingers. He has sheltered her, nothing he has done prepared this child for the life he sold her into.

But keeping her here isn't safe for either one of us. *It's dangerous.* It's been agonizing being so close to her and unable to touch her the way I want to; the way her soul calls to me, begging me to.

We dance the same cat-and-mouse dance every evening when it's time to shower before dinner, I've started to look forward to it. But no matter how badly I want it, I can't bring myself to taint her.

Marcus King is in for quite the surprise when he finally gets her in his grasp. He's expecting a pretty little house-slut, not a pure and innocent angel.

"Why are we still here?" she asks me. We're enjoying the nice weather today, sitting outside on the porch. "I thought I would have been sold into slavery by now."

"Because it isn't safe to take you to Marcus yet."

"And it's going to be safe later?"

She's not a stupid girl, she knows that she's going to get hurt in this transaction.

"Being a mobster's wife isn't really going to be safe—ever. But you already knew that Queen." I put out my smoke in the small brown pottery ashtray on the porch table.

"You should have let me kill myself," she says. "And

when are you ever going to stop calling me that?"

"Then someone would have killed me, so that plan really didn't work for me. And never, you'll always be Queen to me."

"So how long are we still going to be stuck here?" she asks me with a roll of her eyes. "It's getting boring now."

"Boring is good, boring means no one is trying to kill us."

When I look at her, I see all the things I'll never have. I see the future as it could be if I wasn't me and she wasn't her. Queen is a beautiful, deadly reminder of the things that I lost when I joined the Soldati di Sangue.

The idea of us having a life after this is a joke, and a happily ever after would just be against the laws of nature. I kill people for money; a wife and a white picket fence don't go with that. Being near Sophie makes it hard not to wonder what an alternate universe could be like.

After a while in this job, you learn to ignore the guilt. To pretend that this is all just normal. Then, I look at her painting her nails and I am reminded that who I want doesn't deserve me.

When did I start wanting her? Wanting more? I like

being along. That's why this career path was perfect for me—sociopaths don't catch feelings for virginal high school girls with smart mouths. She's making me crazy.

She's a job.

I tell myself the same thing a thousand times a day, but I have become more and more enamored with her each day. We look at each other a little too long for her to just be a job, and no matter what I tell myself, I can't tell my heart not to pound a little harder when I see her smile at me.

"What are you staring at, Sorrow?" she asks.

Her cheeks blush a soft pink and her face is angled slightly down.

"You," I say, not taking my eyes off her.

"Why?"

"Because you—you make me want things I can't have."

"You could have anything you wanted, no one would stop you. You're a serial killer." She shakes her head, like I'm crazy.

"I'm not a serial killer, I am an assassin. It's different. And people say no to me all the time." Arthur says no to me all the time, he treats me like I'm still the boy that came to him a few years ago.

"You wouldn't let me say no to you."

I still wouldn't let her say no to me.

"You can't hurt me."

It's a lie, because if I let her get close, I know this girl could kill me.

"Sorrow?" she starts asking a question, they never seem to end with her.

"Yes, Queen."

"What do you think Marcus will do with me?"

He's going to break you, suck the life out of you and take everything that makes you perfect and destroy it.

"He's going to use the things you love against you. He will try to break your spirit and make you pay for whatever your father did to earn his anger. He will hurt you and when he's done with you—this beautiful innocent carefree you, won't exist anymore."

The truth never hurt anyone; it's better she's prepared for what comes after me. She might fight a little longer if she knows what is going to become of her.

"Wow, don't hold back," she says, wiping stray tears from her cheeks.

She shakes her head and looks away from me, not wanting to show me her vulnerability.

"You're such an asshole. You could have just lied to me, make it seem like my life isn't over for a little while longer."

"Sorry, but honesty never killed anyone."

"Honesty? You want some honesty, Sorrow?" Her voice starts to rise, and I can see the way her left eye twitches. "I've never been kissed before, and until you took your giant wang out and waved it in my face, I'd only ever seen one in my textbooks. I have never had a boyfriend, or a friend for that matter. I'm a virgin, and my stupid father sold me to an old man. An old man that I am terrified of, because I know he won't love me, I know he will rape my body and my mind. So, for fuck's sake, could you just sugar coat the last few days I have left to hope that he's not a fucking monster? I thought I'd at least have felt love once before he took me, but I didn't get the chance. So, let me mourn the loss of my life in denial a little longer—please."

I just stare at her and wonder how it's even possible that no one has ever loved her.

"I'm sorry." I say reaching over the table to put my hand over hers, and this time she doesn't yank it away.

Tonight feels a little different than it has every other night that we've been here—after we spoke on the patio earlier, she shut me out. She left me and went to walk through the gardens, smelling the flowers and touching their petals. I watched her get lost in another world, one where she could have all the things she dreamed of.

Now we are back in our room, there's tension in the air while I shower. The playfulness of the past few days is gone, and this isn't a game any longer. I've had a glimpse inside her soul and now I can't stop wanting to give her things she thinks she'll never have. I want to save her from Marcus, to give her memories that will carry her through the nightmares. I shouldn't want to kiss this little Queen, but fuck me, I do.

She stands there in her panties after I stripped her again, because she's so stubborn.

"Get in the shower, Queen," I say.

Tonight her eyes are open, glaring up into mine with a challenge I shouldn't accept.

"Get in the shower, or I'll drag you in there and make you sorry you didn't listen."

I know she won't listen; I know she wants me to touch her. She begs me with those eyes every time I get close to her.

She holds her breath, just waiting for me to act, and I don't think I can hold back any longer.

I'm about to take something that isn't mine to take.

Her mouth opens slightly, and I see the way her tongue wets her lips. She wants me to kiss her. She needs this as much as I do, I can't resist her teasing any longer.

"Do you want me to kiss those pretty lips, Queen?" She looks up at me, blinking her shiny bright eyes. "If you want me to kiss you, ask me to, I am not a mind reader."

"Kiss me," she says on a breath. "Please."

"No," I smile. "You kiss me."

She looks at me, confused and afraid. I see the way she's thinking about it. If I take the kiss from her, then I'm nothing more than the thief she thinks I am, but if she gives it to me willingly—that's different.

"Don't ever ask for a kiss, Queen. Take one."

"You take it then."

"I won't take anything from you, Queen. So if you want that first kiss, you're going to take it from me."

She sways gently, unsure of what to do. Then, she steps forward, up on her tippy-toes and kisses my smiling lips so softly I can barely feel it. She kissed me, and that gave me all the permission I needed to kiss her back.

Wrapping her in my arms, I pull her small body

against my naked, wet one. One swipe of my tongue and her lips part for me. One taste and I'm addicted. She's not my first kiss, but she's the first kiss that I have managed to feel all the way down in the abyss of my black soul.

When she moans softly into my mouth, I taste her innocence, and it makes me realize I don't want to kiss anyone else ever again. So now my lips belong to this little Queen, and hers to me. I want to be wrapped in her arms, lost in her eyes, I want her and only her—but she's not mine—I can't take her.

She has walked into my heart like she has always belonged there, taken down the walls and set my soul on fire just by taking a single kiss from me. I've been robbed of all my senses as the room spins around us. Biting her bottom lip, I pull away slightly, my forehead still resting against hers.

"Get in the shower, Queen."

"Make me," she hisses back at me.

"If I make you get in that shower, I'm getting in with you, and that kiss won't be your first anything tonight."

"I'm on my period."

She puts her hand on my chest, right where my heart is trying to escape my ribcage and lies straight to my face. The temptation is too much, and I know I am definitely going to take what isn't mine. And I know that I will enjoy every minute of it. Marcus doesn't deserve her—no one does.

"Murder is in my job description, I'm not afraid of a little blood."

Her breath hitches and I see the fear in her eyes as she looks at me, searching for the right answer. Her plan to put me off, to make me stop, has backfired spectacularly. There's more though, she's afraid of this, not of me.

"Are you really a virgin, little Queen? Is that what you're afraid of, that my big cock will ruin you?" I grind against her, making her aware of what she's done to me.

She nods, not looking at me now, embarrassed by her purity.

"It's just a little extra blood then, nothing to worry your pretty head about. Don't panic Queen, I'll ruin you thoroughly before Marcus ever touches you."

Her eyes close as she tries to avoid my stare, I can feel her heartbeat under my fingers as I wrap them around her slender throat. Walking her backwards into the shower.

"You're going to hurt me, aren't you?" she stumbles

on her words; she has nowhere to go.

She's trapped, my body keeping her pinned against the wall.

"Oh, I promise you I am going to hurt you, Queen, but I'll kiss it all better afterwards."

I remove her bra and toss it to the shower floor before sliding those lacy knickers down her perfect legs. Throwing my towel over the top of the shower door, I turn the water on again and turn my attention to worshiping her body now that I can touch it without restraint.

One kiss wasn't enough, I need to kiss every inch of her skin, there's no part of her I don't want to touch. I start with her lips and kiss my way down her neck, slowly tasting her sweetness.

My hands cup her heavy breasts, making her sigh, "Sorrow, please."

"Please what, Queen?" I ask her, stopping to look into her eyes. "Do you want me to stop?"

"No, no, please don't stop. I want it to be you, not him."

She wants me to deflower her, to take her innocence and keep it for myself. I should say no, I should stop—she deserves better than me. But I can't, just touching her wrecks me in a way I can't control.

"Please Sorrow, I want you to have all my firsts, not him."

What are you doing, Tristan? You're going to end up dead.

"Don't fall in love with me, Little Queen," I say as I kiss my way down her chest, falling to my knees. "That would be foolish and dangerous. I'll let you pretend, I'll make it all feel so good, that you'll have memories to make the dark days light, but it's not real. You can't fall in love. I'll know—and I'll stop."

My words are as much for her as they are for the part of me that is melting every minute I'm alone with her. My kisses get hungrier, she tastes so good; I want to devour her. I leave hickeys on her thighs where I suck and bite at the soft flesh; she throws her head back and in a brazen moment puts her hands in my hair.

"Stop me, Queen, because there's no way I'm going to stop myself now." I say, lifting her leg over my shoulder opening her up to me.

When I look up, she's covering her face with her hands.

"What's wrong, Queen?"

"I'm embarrassed," she says, still covering her face.

"Of what? You're gorgeous. You don't need to be embarrassed."

"You're so close to it, you're looking there."

"I'm about to kiss you there, and you're going to forget all about being embarrassed and enjoy it."

"You're what?" she sounds mortified.

I don't let her think about it anymore before I let myself taste her.

"Stop," she pushes my head away. "Please stop, I can't."

Getting up off the floor, I turn off the water; she can come back and wash later. Wrapping my arms around her, I carry her, soaking wet, to the bed. Putting her down, I hover over her, my dick hard from just the smallest taste of her.

"I want you so badly, Queen. I shouldn't—but I do."

She's looking into my eyes now, and I can see the fear, the hesitation, but also there's a look of desire and need that matches mine.

"I want you too, I'm sorry." She covers her face, turning away from my gaze.

"You don't have to be sorry. If you don't want this—any of it—I'll go back to the shower and take care of myself. I'm not going to force you."

"I want it. I want you, Sorrow."

I move so I'm lying beside her, and I turn her onto

her side so I can kiss her again. Our wet bodies sticking to the cotton sheets. I can't keep my hands off of her, she's like putty molding to my touches. When I slide my hand between her legs, softly exploring her delicate folds, she moans and buries her head in my chest.

"Have you ever been fingered before?"

"N-no," she stutters against me, still not looking at me.

"I'm going to make you feel so good, Queen, trust me. Look at me."

She tilts her head up so she can see me, and I slide one finger slowly into her, catching her cry with a deep kiss. Letting her get used to the feeling before I move it, a sublime thrill runs through me when her walls clenched tight around my finger.

"You feel like heaven, Queen," I whisper in her ear. "I'm never going to want to stop touching your pussy."

She squirms at my dirty words, only making my dick harder for her.

"Th-that—it feels good," she says, rolling her hips into me now as I stroke her clit and move my finger over her g-spot.

She lifts her leg so it's wrapped over my thigh, opening herself up to my touch, losing her mind and shedding her inhibitions to me. I collect them as memories, because I know I can't keep her, so I will keep this moment stored away in my mind always. Her cheeks burn flaming red as her body begins to shudder with the beginning of an orgasm, but her shyness and inexperience stops it before it truly starts.

"So shy," I murmur, tracing my fingers feather light down her side, caressing back around to brush over the sensitive flesh I just left.

"You shouldn't be shy, you're beautiful, Queen."

"I'm not," she shakes her head, and tries to look away, but I pin her with just a look.

Shifting so she can feel my dick slide against her wetness, I keep looking at her, waiting for her to stop me. Because this is too good to be real.

"Kiss me, Sorrow," she says as the head of my cock rests at her entrance.

This time I do kiss her, I hold her face and kiss her so she loses her breath, then I slide my tip into her slowly before bucking my hips and pushing myself the rest of the way in. I let go so I can hear the sound of her cry. The echo of her lost youth rips through the room and my chest, it wrenches me open and bares all my demons. That sound forces me to pull out and slam back into her with an uncontrolled, unbridled desire.

When I feel her nails digging into me, and I hear her begging for mercy, it only drives me deeper into her. The wails turn to moans, and slowly her stiffness softens until she's pliable and lets me melt into her.

"Oh, Sorrow!"

"Are you okay?" I ask her, slowing down, but never stopping.

"Oh my God, yes! Yes, don't—don't stop. Please!"

"Never," I lean over and capture her lips in mine again.

Merging my promises with her fears and breaking all the rules, I fuck her. Dare I say it, I make sure she feels loved just this once. I bleed emotions I didn't know were inside me, letting them crawl into the small space between us and glue our jagged edges together.

Panting, her chest rises and falls quickly, and I know that she is close. I hold on a little longer, wanting to make sure that she finds her release before I do. As soon as her moans grow louder again, I know that she is right on the precipice.

Losing control, and my mind, I thrust into her until she comes. I pulse my release deep inside her as a fierce growl rips from me. I collapse on top of her, kissing her neck, all the way up to her face. Still buried inside her, I try telling her things with my kiss.

I'm sorry I hurt you. I'm sorry I lost control. I fucking love you.

That last thought stops me dead. I stiffen and pull out, rolling onto the bed beside her.

"Did you just—?! Inside me?" she shrieks, her voice shaking.

"Yes, I did." *Fuck! I did.*

"What do we do now?" she asks me, her voice a soft whisper.

I don't have a good answer, there's no way to change how this ends now.

"We run, now we run. Because there's no way in hell I am going to give you up, and that means I am a walking dead man."

My little Queen puts her face in the crook of my neck, her breath tickles and comforts me. When she's near, the sadness lifts. It's as if she's the sun burning away the mist of my sorrows.

"I'm not very fast," she says, breathy and light, like she hasn't comprehended how fucking fucked we are right now.

I just defiled the virgin bride of a mob king. I stole

her heart and her body. The universe just showed me love and grief all in the same moment. As I celebrate the love I feel for Sophie, I already begin mourning the inevitable loss of it too. She doesn't understand it yet, but we will both end up dying for this love.

How could I have been so foolish?

CHAPTER 6

Queeen

I'm so stupid. What we did, it shouldn't have happened. Not because I didn't want it, but because now I know exactly what I am going to be missing out on when I am with—no. I can't even think of it; of him.

"Why did you do that? What if I get pregnant? He'll know that it's not his. He'll *kill* you!" I'm rambling, but the thick cloud of desire that was blocking my sanity has dissipated and my anxiety is working overtime.

"I don't care what will happen to me, I need to keep you safe from him."

"Well, *I* care about what happens to you."

The words fly out of my mouth before my brain

realizes what is happening.

He looks at me with a question in his stare. Not as if he thinks I'm lying, more like he is questioning how I would care about him enough to want to protect him.

"How are you going to do that; save me, I mean? Doesn't your friend know where we are?"

"My friend?" he asks, a look of confusion on his face.

"Whoever it is you're always on the phone with," his face falls slightly. "What's wrong?"

"He does."

"So then, where are we headed next?"

"I have no fucking idea," he looks at me like he's about to deliver my death sentence.

That certainly wasn't the answer that I was expecting. He's been so sure of himself and what he needed to do this entire time. Whatever is happening has to be incredibly serious in order to shake him like that.

We're interrupted by the sound of his phone buzzing, and I don't miss the slight flash of fear that dances in his eyes as he looks at the screen.

"Your *friend*?" I ask him.

"Yeah. We have to get out of here; fast," he throws his clothes on and tells me to do the same.

Once I'm dressed, we gather what few items we've collected over the past two weeks.

"Where are we going?" I ask him.

I'm trying to stay calm, but if this was the safest place for us to be right now, then I'm not exactly sure why we're leaving.

"One of my brother's houses. I'm just not sure which one yet. I'll figure it out on the way."

"You have brothers?"

"Queen? We'll talk about it in the truck. Okay?" He stares at me, trying to keep the irritation off of his face.

I nod and within five minutes we're in the truck and on the road.

Thank goodness we're leaving at night; the dark sky provides us with a blanket of protection. It still isn't enough to make me calm down about the fact that we're being hunted. I want to ask Sorrow about his brothers again. He hasn't opened up to me about anything personal in all the time that we were at the bed-and-breakfast. We mostly talked about me except at night when he would strip me down before sending me into the shower.

My head is spinning and I am having a hard time coming to terms with what is real and what isn't. Did

Sorrow really just make me scream and writhe beneath him? Did he actually tell me that he needs to keep me safe because he has no intention of handing me over to Marcus? Is he risking his life, his future, for me?

Fuck, did he really just come in me?

I can't let myself think of it. I'll want to climb in his lap and make him touch me again, just like he did back in the room.

"Breathe, Queenie," he says to me from the driver's seat. "You worry very loudly. Everything will be okay. I promise."

"How can you say that? This entire time you've been telling me how evil and horrible and well-connected Marcus is. How I need to get over the fact that my life is over because there is no hiding from him. Now, all of a sudden, you've decided that I'm worth keeping—"

"No, don't do that. You've always been worth it. My heart has always known it. It just took my brain a little longer to catch up."

"And, apparently, for our circumstances to become more dire." Why did I say that? "I'm sorry. I didn't mean that."

I don't know why I am discrediting his admission.

"It's okay, I didn't really give you a reason to feel otherwise before this," he says.

He places his hand on my leg and rubs my skin gently with his thumb.

"Queenie," he starts.

I wait for him to continue, but I can tell he doesn't know what to say. His demeanor has softened in the time that we've been together. I smile a little to myself, fond of the new nickname he's given me.

"It's fine," I say.

"No, it's not fine. None of this is fine. This is a huge fucking mess, and it's all my fault. I'm single-handedly ruining your life. Things are going to be so much worse for you now. I shouldn't be running with you."

I can't think of what I want to say. I'm terrified to be delivered to Marcus. I'm terrified of being on the run. What happens when Sorrow gets tired of having me around? I am just a little girl, and he is a man with needs that I don't know if I am ever going to be able to fulfil.

How does that make him any different from Marcus?

I don't truly know Sorrow, not yet. But I know enough about him to understand that if he wanted to hurt me, he would have done it by now.

"I don't know what the right thing to do is, Queenie. I don't want to give you up, but the second I decided to take you, I sealed your fate. When Marcus finds us, because he *will* find us, we're both good as dead. I can't let that happen to you."

"I want to be on the run with you, risking my life," I plead with him. "As hard as it's going to be, it's still better than being locked up somewhere; property of Marcus King. I'd rather have a short life full of passion and adventure, than a long life full of terror and pain."

"We can't. I have to take you to Arthur. If I do that, if I take you there, then no one needs to know about any of this, and your life will be spared. You will be delivered to Marcus and—"

I remove my seatbelt as quickly as possible and reach for the door handle.

"What are you doing?" he asks, fear laced in his voice.

Pulling on the handle, I let the door fly open as we speed down the country road that we're on.

"Queenie! No!" he grabs my wrist as he slams on the breaks.

The truck skids off the road and comes to a stop on the grass. I hop out of the truck and run as fast as I can, but it's not fast enough. I feel his presence just before I feel his arms capture me from behind.

"Queenie," he says, winded from the chase and the adrenaline. "What the fuck were you thinking?"

"I was thinking that you're the most selfish son-of-a-bitch that I've ever met in my entire life. You fuck me and then pass me off to my future *husband*," I sob. "Sorrow, if you take me there, so help me God, I *will* kill myself. And then what will this have all been for? Fucking nothing!"

"No! That's not it at all! I want you. I want you so bad it hurts."

"You're a fucking liar! Just like my parents!"

"Okay, it's okay," he whispers in my ear. "I'm sorry. I'm *so* fucking sorry, Queen."

Standing, wrapped in his arms, the sobs don't stop. I'm shaking uncontrollably as they wrack my body. He loosens his grip a little and turns my body around so I am facing him. Running his thumbs under my eyes, he wipes my tears away.

"I'm scared, Sorrow."

"Me too, but I'll never let anything happen to you," he says.

I place my arms around his neck and kiss him. He runs his hands down my body and I jump into his arms, wrapping my legs around his waist. With our lips still firmly locked together, he walks us back toward the truck and props me up against the bumper.

CHAPTER 7

Sorrow

"Help me to be brave. Prove to me that you want me," she says to me, breaking our kiss.

I'm so stupid. I don't know what I was thinking. I just want to keep her safe, but she's right. She's no safer *with* Marcus than she is *not with* Marcus. It took her nearly throwing herself out of a moving vehicle for me to realize it.

"You're already brave, Queen. And I fucking want you like I've never wanted anything else in my sad, sorry life." I say dipping my head down.

I pull her panties to the side and dive my tongue in between her folds.

"Oh…" she sighs with pleasure as she places her hands on my head.

She lies back, her feet planted flat on the hood, her legs fall to the side. I work my tongue, licking her, devouring her as if it's my last meal. So help me, it very well could be. I want to make sure that it's good for her. Everything that I do for the rest of my life will be done with her in mind.

I'm not stupid enough to think that Marcus will never catch up with us. He will, eventually. Until then, I will make every fucking second of every fucking day amazing for this girl.

I pull her body toward the edge of the hood as I stand up. I lick my thumb and my forefinger before taking her clit and squeezing gently. I receive a sharp intake of breath in response and it brings a smile to my face.

"Do you feel brave yet, Queenie?"

"No, I need more, Sorrow."

"I'll give you everything, Queenie."

Once we get back into the car, I start thinking about where we can go. Which of my brothers would be willing to take us in right now? Gawain immediately comes to mind. He just went to hell and back with Megan. He will be able to relate. He's close to Arthur, but I can trust him not to give us up. I need her to feel safe. I never feel safer than I do when I'm with my brothers.

"Where will we go?"

"One of my brother's houses." I don't go into too much detail, the less she knows the better.

"Where does he live?"

"New Orleans; most of my brothers live there."

"How many brothers do you have?"

"Eight," her eyes open in shock, but her expression is quickly replaced by a yawn. She's exhausted, I'm sure, from the escape just as much as from the multiple orgasms she had this evening.

"Why don't you rest? We have a long drive ahead of us."

She lays down across the bench seat and places her head in my lap. I thank God that my dick is resting comfortably on my other leg, otherwise she would have a very hard pillow to lay on. I take the wheel in one hand, placing the other on her head. I run my fingers through her hair gently and before I know it, her breathing has evened out and she's fast asleep.

I knew she was tired. She slept the remaining seventeen hours of our journey, barely even moving when I got out to pump the gas; twice. Fucking big trucks and their shitty gas milage. Luckily, I have cash, so there is no paper trail. I just hope that there weren't any cameras in either of the bumfuck town gas stations where we stopped.

When we get to Gawain's house, I tell Queenie to stay in the truck. I want to gauge his reaction to just me before I bring her in on this. Stepping up to his door, I knock firmly. Listening carefully, I hear footsteps approach the door. I can tell that he is looking out the peephole, cursing me for standing there on his doorstep.

"Gawain, I need your help."

Suddenly, the door opens and I am face-to-face with a very angry Gawain.

"Tristan, what the fuck are you doing here?"

"I didn't know where else to go. I knew that you would be able to help. You will understand what I'm going through."

"I have no fucking idea what you're talking about. All I *know* is that you're supposed to be hidden away, anywhere other than here, with Marcus King's bride."

"Yeah, well, our plans changed unexpectedly."

"You're a dead man walking. There is no way that this is going to end well for either of you. Now, here you are at my house, pulling Megan and me into a very dangerous situation."

He looks past me to the Tahoe in his driveway. To where Queenie is. I feel a wave of protectiveness come over me and a growl escapes from my throat.

"If you think you're going to come here, put our lives in danger because you couldn't do your job *again*, and then *growl* at me on my own doorstep, you're fucked in the head." Gawain barks.

The comment that he made about fucking up another job hits me hard. I try not to let it show, but am unsuccessful.

"Tristan, I'm sorry," he sighs. "I didn't have any right to say that."

"No, you did. It's fine. Look, I just thought that you, out of everyone, would understand. After what went down with Megan—"

She appears at the door as soon as her name leaves my mouth.

"Tristan, hi! How are you?" she asks me.

"Hanging in there, what about yourself?"

She looks up at Gawain and he gives her a wink.

"We're great, thank you. What's going on?"

It's interesting to me how she has walked into the conversation as if she's been commanding it the entire time. She's come a long way since Gawain first found her.

Gawain rolls his eyes with an exaggerated sigh, but I know that's his consent to tell her what's happened.

"I fell in love," I begin.

A look of happiness appears on her face for a moment until she realizes that it's not mirrored on my own. "With Marcus King's future wife."

The smile on her face drops quickly as the words spill out of my mouth.

"Is that who is in the truck?" Her head nods in the direction of the Tahoe.

"Look, I'm sorry to come here like this. I just don't know where else to go. I understand if you don't want us here."

I've never felt as humble as I do right now. But when it comes to Sophie, I can't afford to be lackluster with my actions. It's not just me anymore. I have someone else to think about now. Someone who's life I value greater than my own.

Gawain looks at Megan, unsure of what to do. I understand what he's feeling. It's not just about him anymore. He needs to think about Megan now, just like I need to think about Sophie.

Megan returns his glance with a sympathetic look.

"You would do the same for me."

Gawain rolls his eyes, knowing that she speaks the truth.

"The two of you can stay here for a little while. I won't say anything to Arthur. But don't think of this as a vacation. Use your time here to come up with a plan to save both of your asses. And do it before Arthur finds out. I don't want to be the next person on his shitlist."

I nod to him and return to the truck to get Sophie out. As I reach forward to open the door, I hear Megan speak next to me.

"Hi! I'm Megan," she says to Sophie.

"Hey," is all my Queenie can say as she steps down out of the truck.

"You'll be safe here. Gawain is kind of a stickler for security."

"Thank you for letting us stay," she says, "it really means a lot. I'm sorry to put you out like this."

"Don't even think of it. We're happy to have you."

CHAPTER 8

Queen

We've been here for a week and, while Gawain is a little scary, it's been perfect. Megan is a sweetheart, and she has been able to help me forget the hell that I'm actually in. As wonderful as it's been, I haven't been able to enjoy it as much as I want to, knowing that I'm still putting all of these people in serious danger.

Sorrow and Gawain often shut themselves away in the study to "talk business" as Sorrow says. I want to know what's happening. What the latest news is. Are my parents still alive? Is anyone still out there looking for me; anyone *other than* Marcus King?

There have been a few times I've caught the two

of them in hushed conversation, talking about another one of their brothers; Gareth. Apparently, Gareth lost the love of his life a year ago and hasn't been the same ever since. I can tell Sorrow is hurting deeply for him. I know he wants to go to him, to be there for him, but he can't because he's stuck here with me.

"Keep it down over there," Sorrow says.

His voice vibrates through this chest, tickling my ear as my head rests there. He always knows when there is something bothering me. He reaches over and grabs me underneath of my arms, pulling me on top of him.

"What's wrong, Queenie?" he asks, tucking my hair behind my ear.

I grab his hand before he has a chance to pull it away. Kissing his palm, I link our fingers together, not wanting to break our contact.

"I don't know. I just—" I have no idea what's wrong or what I'm trying to say. "I'm just scared. I don't like the fact that I'm putting all of you in danger."

"Queenie, you're not putting anyone in danger. If anything, *I'm* the one doing that, okay? And don't worry, Gawain will throw us out when he gets tired of us being here."

I want to smile, but I can't. I'm too nervous. My stomach is tied in knots laced with guilt. When I don't respond, Sorrow pushes me off him and throws me onto my back next to him. He grips my wrists in one of his hands, holding them in place above my head.

"If you can't let it go, then I'll just fuck you until you forget whatever it is you're worried about."

"Sorrow, stop," I plead, breaking free from his grip. I place my hands on his shoulders, pushing him away gently. "Be serious."

His entire body stills as his stare catches me, paralyzing me with feelings of fear and lust.

"I've never been more serious in my entire life, Queenie. Put your hands above your head, grab hold of the headboard and hold on tight."

For a second it's hard to find my Sorrow in his stare. The fierce silver stare looking back at me is one that I've not seen from him before. I lift my arms and rest them on the mattress above my head.

"Whatever you do, don't let go."

He sits up and grips the t-shirt that I am wearing between his hands before ripping it into pieces, and I watch them fall down onto the mattress. His hands land on my breasts with a squeeze to each. His right hand skirts up my body, stopping at my neck, which floods my lust with fear, while the fingers on his other hand find my nipple and roll it between them.

"Have you forgotten your worries yet? Have you let them go?"

"No," I pant.

I would have said no even if I had. My growing fascination with Sorrow and his talented tongue and skilled fingers is increasing still.

"Good," he replies before he scoots himself down my body and dives into my pussy tongue first.

"Oh!" I cry out as he drives both his tongue and his fingers into me. "Oh my God!"

I let go of the headboard and place one of my hands on his head, egging him on. With the other hand, I grab a pillow and place it over my face to stifle my screams of ecstasy.

He makes me come endlessly until he has completely and thoroughly fucked my worries away.

Sorrow and I spend the rest of the day in bed. Sleeping, touching, caressing. This day has been a dream. We needed it. I know that we won't be here much longer, and I am not sure when we will have another chance to be so happy and carefree.

Lifting the covers away from my body, I carefully

climb out of bed while trying not to wake him. I've never seen him as peaceful as he is when he's sleeping. I tip-toe into the bathroom and close the door behind me. As good as Sorrow has made me feel today, I also feel dirty; and a little sticky in a few places. A shower sounds amazing right about now.

As I let the spray of water wash away the evidence of my pleasure, doubt begins creeping back in. I wish that there was something that I could do to fix this. I hate that there are so many people getting caught in the crosshairs just because of me. They don't know me; I'm no one. An insignificant casualty in a war between a spineless father and a sadistic, power-hungry tyrant.

My father cared more about his social status and possessions than his family. Now, Marcus King gets to reap my father's spoils; me.

Lost in thought, I'm not sure how long I've been in the shower, but the water is beginning to turn cold. I shut it off and grab a towel to wrap myself in before returning to the bedroom. I must have been gone for a while because Sorrow is gone when I get there.

I look through Sorrow's bag, grabbing another t-shirt and a pair of his boxers. I have every intention of lying down and going back to sleep until I hear yelling coming from downstairs. I run from the room, scared at what I may find when I get there.

"What the fuck do you mean you told Arthur?" Sorrow is screaming at Gawain when I make it to the study.

"There was no way I was going to be able to keep this from him; not without screwing myself and Megan over, anyway. I told you when you got here that this was temporary."

Fuck. I knew that we weren't welcome here; that *I'm* not welcome here.

"I told you I wasn't treating this like a free-ride. I've been wracking my brain trying to figure out how to get us out of this mess. I. Love. Her. This isn't just a fling. This isn't something that is just going to go away. She isn't some random that I'm going to discard when I'm done with her. I will *never* be done with her."

"I know that. I can tell. You're, *different* around her," Gawain sighs. "Listen, Arthur said he's calling a truce. He needs all of us there for Gareth. He needs *you* there for Gareth, especially."

Sorrow stands in front of his brother with his arms crossed and his jaw twitching. Pursing his lips, I can tell that he doesn't know what to do. He's struggling and all I want to do is run to him, but I don't think that he would appreciate that right now.

"While we're out there, take Arthur aside and talk to him about all of this. If *anyone* can help you out of this situation, he will be your best bet."

Walking away from the study, I hurry back up the steps before I get caught eavesdropping. I barely make it into bed before he walks, defeated, through the door. Without looking at me, he walks into the bathroom and showers. I lay down on the bed and close my eyes, falling into a deep sleep before he's even finished showering.

CHAPTER 9

Sorrow

Today I said goodbye to one of the best people I know. Gareth was not only my brother, but my best friend. We looked out for one another. We were closer with one another than our other brothers. My only comfort is knowing that his truth was brought to light, and he had accepted his fate.

We got here a week ago and have been staying in his house while he stayed at Bentlee's. Arthur didn't come looking for us, and Gareth sure as hell wasn't going to give up our location either. Arthur isn't stupid though, I'm sure he knows exactly where we are.

He questioned me prior to Gareth finding us. I

thought for sure he wasn't going to let me leave until I gave up our location. I'm shocked that he didn't. He may have been too affected by the loss of Gareth to push the issue, but whatever the case may be, I'm not going to look a gift horse in the mouth.

We will be leaving today. I need to get Sophie somewhere safe before he changes his attitude or Marcus finds out that the entire brotherhood is in Vegas and comes looking for a fight. We're ditching the Tahoe and catching a ride back to New Orleans with Seth and Leeann. His truck is a lot bigger than ours, anyhow. She and Sophie actually have a lot in common, and I think it could help both of them to have each other to talk to.

I'm jolted awake as Seth drives over a rocky area in the road. At least that's what I thought it was. Once my vision clears a little, I see Sophie with her head between my legs and her lips around my cock. The sight of her, the feel of her tongue as she runs it over the sensitive skin there, has me ready to explode. I try my hardest to keep quiet, but can't help the strangled moan that comes from deep within. Sophie removes her beautiful lips from around my cock and puts her finger to them, shushing me.

I nod to her and she cocks an eyebrow at me as she sticks her tongue out and licks the precum from the tip of my cock. Just then, the truck begins to slow and we both lift our heads just in time to see Seth turning into the parking lot of a local fast food place.

"We're going to grab something to go. Are you guys coming?"

Sophie's hand never lets go of its grip on my cock and she continues to work it as Seth parks the truck.

"No—" I try to get out, but my voice came out making me sound like I was going through puberty all over again. I clear my voice and try again. "No. We're good."

Sophie sits next to me, smiling slightly, still rubbing my cock in her beautiful hand.

"Okay," Seth raises his eyebrow at me, knowingly. "We *won't* be long."

"Take your time," I shout after him just before he closes the driver's side door.

No sooner that it's closed, I tackle Sophie down onto the backseat of the truck. I pull down on the tank top that she has on, pulling the cups of her bra down as I go. Her tits pop out and are on full display. My hands move all over her. Her tits, her ass, her pussy. There is not one square inch of her skin that I don't touch.

"Do you trust me?" I ask, licking the skin that's covered by her generous cleavage.

"Of course."

I pull her up and remove my pants. Then, I settle myself in the middle of the back seat.

"Straddle me, but face the front seat."

She looks apprehensive and starts tucking her tits back into her bra.

"What if someone sees?"

I reach a hand over, cupping her cheek for reassurance.

"You said you trusted me."

She takes a deep breath as I reach out and free her perfect breasts again. Capturing one of her delicious peach nipples in my mouth, I reach out and pull her shorts and panties down her legs.

"Straddle me, Queenie," I demand.

She places one leg on the other side of me and twists so she is facing the front of the truck. Before she has a chance to sit down, I capture her by the leg just under her ass and hold her in place, legs spread open wide for me.

"Sorrow! What are you doing?" She screams and I

can contain the devilish smile that appears on my lips as I press them to her slit. Sticking my tongue out, I lick a straight line from her clit to her ass.

Her sudden intake of breath spurs me on and my tongue slithers back down to her opening. I wrap my other hand around my cock and pump it a few times while I fuck her with my tongue.

"Oh, God. Oh, God," she pants.

"I think of myself as more of a devilish type," I respond her to her, removing my hand from her leg and lowering her down onto my cock.

I guide her hips in a circular motion, helping her relax in this position.

"Shit—" she mutters. "I don't—it hurts—"

I stop my movements and lift her off carefully.

"This isn't over, turn around."

She rearranges herself until she is facing me and I enter her once again.

"How's that?"

"Better, thank you,"

"I'd do anything for you, Queenie."

"Please, call me Sophie," she begs.

I grab onto her hips once again as I begin to drive into her from beneath. Her tits are bouncing in my face, teasing me, begging to be bitten. I grab one of them between my teeth and bite down gently.

Then, I suck on it to ease the sting. My thrusts continue growing more rapid each time I enter her. It's not long before she's crying out her release. As soon as I feel her muscles contract around me, I shoot my cum deep inside of her. I know I shouldn't. It's a huge risk, nearly as huge as stealing and running from Marcus King.

I can't think about him right now. Not when I'm still balls deep inside of the girl who makes me want to shed my tragic nickname. I do need to figure out a resolution that suits the needs and desires of all parties involved. Before anything unimaginable happens.

CHAPTER 10

Queen

We're almost back to New Orleans. Well, the outskirts, where Seth and Leeann live, anyway.

"Is that one of King's men?" Sorrow asks Seth.

"Fuck. Yeah, I'm pretty sure."

"Are they looking for me? For Queenie?"

I don't hear Seth answer, just a defeated sigh that comes from Sorrow.

"Does King know where you live?" I hear Sorrow ask.

I've been laying down with my eyes closed, nodding off, but not quite sleeping. Leeann is back here with me now too, with Sorrow riding shotgun. I've been listening to him and Seth talk. I'm trying to see if I can catch any bits of his life that he hasn't shared with me yet. Like his name, maybe?

When I hear the mention of Marcus King, my eyes go wide.

"Not to my knowledge," Seth answers. "But don't quote me or anything. I mean, he's Marcus fucking King. They're too fucking close, though. I'm only about five miles from here."

I swallow the lump in my throat as a phone starts ringing.

"Is it him?" Sorrow asks, but I don't hear Seth say anything in response.

"Shit," Sorrow sighs.

Fuck, that doesn't sound good.

"Arthur," Seth says when he answers the phone.

"No, I haven't seen him since Vegas."

"Mmmhmm. Oh. Okay, I'll let you know if I see him."

"What did he say?" Sorrow asks, I can hear the anxiety in his voice.

"T, it's not good, man. King put a hit out on the entire brotherhood. He'll kill anyone on the spot until he gets the girl. The bastard said that if he gets her within the next two days, then he'll remove the hit and she won't be harmed. Otherwise..."

"Fuck!" Sorrow yells, punching the dashboard in front of him repeatedly.

A tear slips from the corner of my eye. I know what I need to do. I've been selfish and have put so many good, innocent people in grave danger. They are not dying because of me.

Sorrow is fast asleep next to me. We made love when we got here, but I haven't been able to fall asleep yet. What Seth said to Sorrow keeps playing in my head on repeat. I can't do this. So many people are being threatened right now, and I can't be the reason behind it. I'm no one. An insignificant little girl. Having to spend the rest of my life with Marcus is a small price to pay compared to people dying.

I take one final glance at Sorrow as my heart twists in pain. I place a gentle kiss on his forehead and carefully climb out of his bed, and his life, forever.

I made it out of Seth's house undiscovered. Luckily,

they didn't catch me watching when he typed in the code to the alarm system. I breathe a sigh of relief that no one caught me and alerted Sorrow. He can't know what I'm doing. He will come after me and get himself killed.

But my sigh of relief is replaced with sinking dread as I start off on the next leg of my journey. I have no idea where Marcus lives, but I know that one of his men was stationed five miles from Seth's house, based on what he told Sorrow in the truck earlier. I have no idea which direction I'm going or if I'm even moving toward or away from him, but I need to find one of his men and turn myself in.

When I've been walking for about an hour, and I think that I won't be able to take one more step, I see some lights up ahead and walk toward them. When I get closer, I see that it's a tiny Italian restaurant. It seems very out of place, but it's the only thing nearby and I am exhausted. Even if they can't help me, I may at least be able to sit down and have a glass of water.

"Excuse me?" I say to the gentlemen sitting at the only occupied table across the room.

One of them is a huge oafy-looking guy. He must be the muscle. The other two look like your typical mobsters; big, meaty dudes with shiny, black hair and bulky jewelry.

They stop their conversation and turn their attention to me.

"What do we have here?" one of them says as he gets up and stalks over to me.

I have never been so terrified before. Not even when Sorrow took me.

Don't even think about him.

"It's not safe for you to be alone at night around here, darlin'."

"Um," I begin.

Come on, Soph. Remember why you're doing this. These guys probably aren't as scary as Marcus King, so suck it up and save your scared little girl bullshit for him.

"I'm looking for Marcus King."

They look at one another and break out into a fit of laughter.

"What the hell kind of business do you have with Marcus King?"

"I'm his fiancée."

That wipes the smiles off their faces. The big oaf I'm talking to reaches out and grabs me under my bicep before dragging me over to the other men at the table.

"Stay here," he tells me, forcing me into a seat between the Jersey Shore rejects.

He walks into a small room behind the kitchen.

"Boss. This one says she's Marcus King's fiancée."

"Bring her to me."

"Get over here, darlin'."

Standing on shaky legs, I walk to where the oaf is standing. He moves out of the way so his boss can have a look at me. He examines me the way a scientist looks at a petri dish, only he's the disgusting one.

"Bring the car around, Luigi. We've got a wedding to save."

CHAPTER 11

Sorrow

"Queenie?" I woke up a minute ago to a cold and empty bed.

I pad into the bathroom to see if Sophie is there, but there is no sign of her and no sign that she has been in there at all this morning.

Something is wrong.

I grab some clothes and head downstairs to look for her. She isn't there, but I find Seth and Leeann.

"Have you guys seen Sophie this morning? She wasn't in bed when I woke up."

"No, I haven't seen her since we got home last night," Leeann says.

I walk around the house calling her name with no response.

"Tristan! Get the fuck in here, man!" I hear Seth scream from the kitchen, and I take off running toward him.

"What? What's wrong?"

"I pulled up the security footage from last night... look."

I tear the tablet from Seth's hands and watch in terror as I see Queenie's figure climb down the front steps and run away from the house.

"What the fuck time was this?!" I shout, not that it matters, it was dark out when she left.

I start hyperventilating.

"I have to go to her, Seth. He—he'll ruin her."

"Tristan, he'll fucking kill you."

"*You don't fucking think I know that?*" I scream at my brother with tears streaming down my face. "I *have* to try for her; for us. She's my everything. There is nowhere she can go that I won't follow. That includes the lair of the Devil himself."

I swerve Seth's car, nearly crashing into the

gatehouse at the edge of King's property.

"My name is Tristan Sorrow." I say as I jump from the car. "Tell Marcus that I'm here and I'm ready for a fight."

The guard at the gate looks at me like I'm on drugs.

"*Move your ass!*" I scream at him.

A few minutes pass by, but it feels like hours. Finally, I see a car approaching from the other side of the fence. I run over there with my hands above my head and wait for his men to get out of the car. I'm greeted by the larger of the two with a hard punch to the face before my world goes black.

I wake with a start as I catch another fist to the face. I'm no longer outside; I am somewhere underground. I look around, trying to focus my eyes, when they land on my innocent little Queenie, shackled to the wall across the room from me.

I look up at her from my spot on the floor, where I'm tethered to the wall, a chain locked around my ankle. She has a cut on her lip and rope burns around her wrists and ankles. He has her in some god-awful, skimpy, white, gauzy fabric dress that barely covers the delicious, sweet spot between her legs. As terrible as she looks, she will always be beautiful to me.

"Sorrow! No! Marcus, please! Stop! Don't hurt him! You said that you wouldn't hurt anyone if I came to you!"

"Poor Sophie, you really are terribly naïve, aren't you? You'll learn soon enough."

I look across the dungeon at her and beg her with my stare to be brave.

"I'm so—sorry, Sophie."

Her cries grow stronger as I call her by her real name.

"Oh, good. You're awake." Marcus says. "The two of you have been very bad. You took something that belongs to me. And then you defiled her. Now? Well, now I have a very expensive payment to collect from each of you for your transgressions."

"I'll do anything you want, okay? Just please let him go," she pleads.

He turns and focuses his attention on her.

"You'll do anything I say, because I say you will. Not because *you* tell me you will. That's not how this works, *wife*."

My eyes shoot to her left hand. I didn't notice the

gleam of gold and diamonds before. Jesus, he moves fast.

"Marcus," I start. "Please. None of this was her fault. I was the one who took her. Please don't punish her for my mistakes.

He responds with brass knuckles to my eye. Spots dance in my vision and I plead with myself not to pass out. By the time the spots disappear, he's on the other side of the room, unbuckling her shackles and removing the poor excuse for a dress from her body. Then he turns her around so she is facing the wall.

Fuck, what is he doing?

"My dear Sophie. You're going to learn that you can't disrespect me and get away with it." He unbuckles his belt and squares up with her, ready to strike. "Hopefully, this is the only time I will have to teach this lesson to you."

Raising his arm into the air, he brings it down on her bare back. The scream that rings through the room, the sight of her skin breaking open, the blood that drips down her back, causes my heart to shatter into a thousand pieces.

"No!" I shout.

She turns around as much as possible and looks at me; her destroyed expression turning the shards of my heart to dust.

"That's one, count them out!"

She takes a shallow, staggering breath before speaking.

"One." She's in so much pain her voice comes out barely more than a whisper.

"What's that, pet? I couldn't quite hear you," he sneers.

"*ONE!*" she sobs.

"Marcus!" I scream. "Give me her punishment. Every last one of them and then give me my own." I plead with him, knowing that it's not going to do any good.

I am a selfish coward for what I've done. She doesn't deserve this, and I sure as fuck don't deserve her.

"Sophie, I'm so sorry for all of this." I pause. "I love you."

Her sobs become stronger the second that her name leaves my lips.

"Setti!" Marcus calls to someone outside of the door and one of his cronies walks in.

"Take her to my room and ready her for me like you did last night. I'll finish her punishment when I'm through here."

"No!" Sophie and I shout at the same time. She turns and runs toward me, but the man gets to her first.

"What is your name? Sorrow, please!" she begs me, her feet planted firmly on the ground, trying her best not to be pulled away. "Please, tell me! I need to know!"

Sophie sobs as hot tears fall from her face. King's man has her in his grasp, and the sight of it feels like a dagger in my heart. She's being carried away, over the shoulder of the oaf that's got a hold on her. She reaches out and her fingers wrap around the stone edge of the doorframe, but just as she gets a grip, she loses it again.

"Tristan!" I scream.

"I love you, Tristan!"

My name manages to escape her lips the second before she disappears from my sight for the last time, ever.

I love you, Sophie.

That's my last thought before King kicks me over so I am flat on my back looking up at him. A tear escapes from my eye. Not out of fear or sadness for myself, but because of what will happen to Queenie.

This is all my fault. I could have saved her from this heartbreak. If I had a little more self-control. If I could have kept my dick and my heart on ice. It still would have been earth shattering, but now it will be utterly unbearable for Sophie. I'm a fucking bastard. Always have been. Always will be.

And I deserve everything that's about to happen to me.

"You fucked with the wrong man," he says as he thrusts a blade into my stomach with vicious force behind it. "And I'm going to take great pleasure in destroying her. When I'm finished, she will be begging for death to claim her."

He removes his knife from my stomach and drives it deep into my heart.

It hurts even more now that I've learned how to let someone into it.

EPILOGUE

One Year Later

Tristan once told me if I managed to kill him, the wrath of eight angry murderers would rain down on me like a hurricane.

He wasn't lying.

Only it wasn't me who killed him. It was Marcus King.

The same man who ripped me open and tore away at my insides until I was nothing but a million different pieces for those same murderers to put back together. There aren't nine brothers in the Soldati di Sangue anymore, but they're just as strong, brutal, and dangerous as ever.

After what went down with Gareth in Vegas, Arthur ordered everyone back to the compound for a mandatory debrief. So, when he got the call from Seth that morning, they were all there, ready to fight for their own.

When they were finally able to infiltrate and successfully take hold of Marcus' compound, they found me tied to Marcus' bed, a shell of my former self. Beaten, bloody and bruised, my dignity ripped from my body. Paralyzed by heartbreak.

King destroyed me, not because of what he did to *me*, but what he did to *Tristan*. He never did make it out of the dungeon that day. He died down there, just like Tristan did. The Soldati di Sangue made sure he paid for his sins with his life.

Just like Tristan did.

I was in the hospital for a long time following the events of that day, but when the physical injuries healed, the emotional ones were still incredibly raw. I didn't want to live after that. I begged and pleaded with the brotherhood to kill me. To put me out of my misery. To send me home to Tristan. But they never listened. They kept telling me that life would get better. That if they were to do as I asked, then Tristan would have died in vain.

It's a truth that I never wanted to accept. I tried to pull away from them, but there was something about each one of the brothers that reminded me so much of Tristan. Every time they would let their "Tristan" show, I would realize exactly how much they meant to me, and the desire to leave would evaporate into nothing.

Tristan was my everything.

He taught me what love looks like. He taught me how to let go, how to be free, how to be brave, and how to fight for what I believe in. He showed me what it's like to have a family that cares about you. He told me that he learned all of those things from his brothers.

Now, each of them is picking up where he left off. They give me advice; they joke around with me, pick on me. I can laugh with them and cry on their shoulders when I need to. They tell me stories about Tristan.

I live with Seth and Leeann. I connect with them more than the others. On nights that I can't sleep, Leeann will come into my room and we'll talk for hours. Sometimes we talk about our lives before we were saved by the men of the Soldati di Sangue. Mostly we talk about how thankful we are and how much better our lives have become because of them.

It's been a year since I lost Tristan. I don't miss

him or love him any less now than I did a year ago. I try not to dwell on what could have been or how much we missed out on since then. Instead, I focus on the time that we did have together and I try to be thankful that we got as much of it as we did.

When Tristan took me that day, he took my heart. It wasn't something that I was ready to give, and I fought hard to keep it from him. But the heart wants what it wants, and I know now that I never had a choice in the matter. My heart was meant for him. It belongs to him.

It will stay with him until the day that I take my last breath and leave this earth behind, forever.

Interconnected standalones that will push your limits, test your one-handed reading technique, and take you into a suspenseful world where men are domineering and dangerous, and their female counterparts are feisty and strong.

Are you ready to take the ride with us?

Beautifully Brutal - Dani René
Vow of Obedience - Brianna Hale
His Salvation - Claire Marta
Ivy's Poison - India R. Adams
Delinquent - Ally Vance
Redemption - Anna Edwards
Valor - Measha Stone
Sorrow's Queen - Ashleigh Giannoccaro
& Murphy Wallace
Inexorable - Jo-Anne Joseph

Sneak Peek

INEXORABLE
JO-ANNE JOSEPH

PROLOGUE

Before

Blood. The price of betrayal and redemption. A life lesson passed down from my father, Luther Calthorpe. He was a legend, a god of his own making, and a redeemer. People shuddered at the sound of his name, yet they bowed at his feet. Luther was the father of organized crime. The man was ruthless and unapologetic. He could crush a man's skull, gouge out his eyes with his bare hands, and not blink an eye. People whispered about him, told stories about the men he'd butchered. But to me, he was just Father. The patriarch of the Calthorpe family, and a man I looked up to. I wanted to instill that kind of fear in people.

My family was one of the oldest, most affluent, and most feared families in New Orleans, where our roots ran deep. We practically owned the city, controlling energy, transportation, and mining to name a few. These were just a few of our endeavours and by the seventies, we'd almost monopolized New Orleans. Nothing happened without us knowing about it. Having that much power also meant that we were untouchable.

I grew up understanding that I was to uphold the dynasty at all costs. That no life was worth risking the family name for. It was no secret that the Calthorpes had more enemies than friends, but our influence was our security, my father said, and that would always be our advantage. A smart man kept his friends close and his enemies even closer, with a gun to their backs, just in case.

By my eighth birthday, Luther had already taught me how to fire a gun and use a knife for its true purpose. Instead of the toy pistols other children my age were playing with, I was gifted my first *Walther*, a replica of the one used by Adolf Hitler.

"The world is not a playground, Arthur, it's a battlefield." My father told me.

I remember the feel of the cold metal when he

placed it in my palms, the excitement I felt that he'd trusted me enough to hand me my first weapon. I aimed it at a 3D, rubber silhouette target dummy in our back garden and pulled the trigger without hesitation. Fear and excitement coursed through my veins at the knowledge that it'd been a loaded weapon. Pride filled me when I looked at the dummy, my bullet lodged dead center in its head. My hand trembled slightly, the beat of my heart pounded in my ears, and I smiled up at my father, who nodded in approval.

His approbation was all I sought, even at that young age. It was not to my mother's bosom to which I ran when I was hurt, but to him where he'd tell me to toughen up, and be a man. A man did not cry over small cuts and bruises. I'd gain many more before my life was done, so I'd best get used to them.

I would stand tall, and suddenly a bruised knee or split lip wouldn't matter much anymore. Luther was my hero, and I wanted nothing more than to be just like him.

I had my first real kill at the age of eleven. Before that, I'd hunted with my father, but it was not the same as taking a human life. A merchant made the mistake of crossing my father, consorting with a sworn enemy of the Calthorpes. He'd risked his life for five hundred thousand dollars which lay beside him on the ground. One of my father's men, Marco Carvalho, intercepted the merchant on his way home with the cash in his hands. He'd fit in the crowd, just a regular businessman, until Marco sunk his metal claws into his forearm. He literally had metal inserted into his hands in place of fingernails. There'd been no fight between the two men; the merchant simply allowed himself to be led. He knew the price for disloyalty.

We stood in the woods that formed the backdrop of our estate in New Orleans. Cherrybark oak trees towered above us, the sound of the small stream that trickled through our property bringing a sense of calm that was in contrast to what was about to happen.

These woods were where my father and I hunted during deer season. The image of Luther dragging a carcass he'd shot with a strongbow came to mind, and I wondered if Marcus would drag this man away in much the same way. The furnace in the basement was already awake; the dragon I called it. It would engulf this man soon enough.

The man kneeled on the ground, his shoulder-length black hair, which had been in a ponytail when he arrived, now hung in clumps over his face. Sweat dripped from his brows, and his body quivered. Blood oozed from the spot where Marcus's claws had gripped him, tainting his white shirt. Large brown eyes pleaded up at my father who stood straight-backed watching him with disinterest.

"He's yours, Arthur." My father said. The man looked me right in the eye, begging me silently, praying to the god he served for another chance. *But the Calthorpes don't do second chances, and around here, there was no god but us.*

"Look him in the eye when you do it." Luther's voice was sturdy, sure, as he stood beside me, his steady hand placed with casual ease on my shoulder. When I felt my hand tremble as it wrapped around the revolver, he leaned down, and I will never forget what he whispered in my ear. "Today you choose, Arthur. Conquer or yield?"

I watched the tears stream down the man's face, and as I pulled the trigger, aiming for his forehead, I chose my destiny. His body slumped to the ground, his brains spread out like a crimson pillow on the ground beneath his head. I stepped closer, wanting a better view. It felt anticlimactic for some reason, so looking down at him, I smiled and shot him once more through the heart because it felt right. I felt invincible. Like I could lead an army to war like in the movies I watched.

"You enjoy this too much." My father cheered in the background. His partner and best friend, Stephen Castello, clapped him on the back and cast a wink my way. Stephen's son, my best friend, Daniel, shivered beside his father. His eyes were wide with horror at the sight before him. He'd always been a weak one. I grinned at him, calling for him to come and get a closer look. He shied away, glancing from the gun in my hands to my face.

"Come," I commanded, and our fathers looked on in amusement. "Come see what I've done, Danny."

He stepped forward slowly, his feet crushing the dry autumn leaves beneath his feet. He stood beside me, his body vibrating. I could smell it. Fear, the scent strong and heady. He looked everywhere but at the body that lay at our feet.

"The day will come when you will have to make the same choice. I only hope you'll make the right one," I whispered.

I looked down at the still body. There was still blood coursing through those veins and arteries. Then I shot the man's leg, the one closest to Danny's feet, even our fathers shook at the sound, then laughed. Danny covered his ears, and when the blood began to pour out on his shoe, he bent at the waist and started to vomit all over the man's body. I finally stepped away, washing my hands in a dish of water one of my father's men had brought. I wiped my gun, slipping it into the holster.

"That boy is a king," Stephen told my father, and when I saw the pride in Luther's eyes, I believed I truly was. I was a king. I would kill and maim and destroy.

I never knew the name of the man I'd killed or the names of several others who followed in the years after him, but I remember all their eyes. I remember the smell of their fear and the ecstasy of seeing their lives seep slowly from them.

I feared nothing, even death itself, until Guinevere Tudor.

Acknowledgments

Thank you so much to Ashleigh Giannoccaro for collaborating with me on this story. I love Sorrow and Queen! Thank you for trusting me to help you tell their story!

Another huge thank you to Dani René for including me in such an incredible project. It's been a dream of mine for a while to work on a series like this, so thank you for helping that dream come true!

My Beta Readers – Alicia Stubbs, Michelle McGinty, Jamie Johnson, Ashley Allen, Kirsty Adams, and Patty Walker – Double the brainpower behind the story needs a few extra sets of eyes. A big thank you for all of your help! Sorrow and Queen were in very good hands!

My Street Team – For always working your asses off to get my name out there. My notifications are constantly blowing up because of you and each and every one of them brings a smile to my face and tears to my eyes. Knowing how much you all support me means everything in the world! You're the best!

To my family – thank you always for your love and support. I wouldn't be able to do what I do without you.

ALSO BY
MURPHY WALLACE

The Wildheart Duet
(Dark Romantic Suspense)
Stolen Love
With Love
Box Set

The Dirty Heroes Collection
(Dark Fairytale Retelling)
Bound in Sacrifice

Driven World
(Contemporary Romantic Suspense)
Octane

ABOUT
MURPHY WALLACE

Murphy Wallace is an International Bestselling Author with works in several different genres, but mostly in Dark Romantic Suspense.

Her heroines are caring, strong, and independent and will protect their loved ones with everything they have. Her heroes? They can't get enough of their ladies! These men embrace their wild love and sassy attitudes, and if you even think about crossing them, they won't hesitate to deliver dangerous retribution.

When Murphy is not writing or getting in touch with her inner child at Disney World, she enjoys reading, coloring, and spending time with family. She currently resides in a small Eastern Florida town with her husband, who doubles as her best friend, and their two boys.

She has a cat named Maisy who is her constant writing partner.

FIND MURPHY ONLINE

Website: https://murphywallace.net
VIP Club: http://bit.ly/MurphysVIPs
Profile: http://bit.ly/MurphyWallace
Page: http://bit.ly/AuthorMurphyWallace
Group: http://bit.ly/MurphysLovers
Instagram: http://bit.ly/InstaMurph
TikTok: http://bit.ly/MurphyTok
BookBub: http://bit.ly/MurphyBB
Twitter: http://bit.ly/MurphyTwitter
Goodreads: http://bit.ly/MWGoodreads
Amazon: https://bit.ly/MurphyZon

Made in the USA
Middletown, DE
05 May 2022